THE QUANGLE WANGLE'S HAT

THE QUANGLE WANGLE'S HAT

By *Edward Lear* *Illustrated by* *Janet Stevens*

Voyager Books

Harcourt Brace & Company

San Diego New York London

First Voyager Books edition 1997
Voyager Books *is a registered trademark of
Harcourt Brace & Company.*

*Library of Congress Cataloging-in-Publication Data
Lear, Edward, 1812–1888.
The Quangle Wangle's hat/by Edward Lear;
illustrated by Janet Stevens.—1st ed.
p. cm.
Summary: Fanciful creatures, including the Stork, the Duck,
the Owl, the Frog, and the Fimble Fowl come to build their
homes on the Quangle Wangle's commodious hat.
ISBN 0-15-264450-4
ISBN 0-15-201478-0 (pbk.)
1. Children's poetry, English.   [1. Nonsense verses.
2. Animals—Poetry.   3. English poetry.]
I. Stevens, Janet, ill.   II. Title.
PR4879.L2Q3   1988*

821'.8—dc19   87-29616

F E D C B A

Printed in Singapore

*The illustrations in this book were done in watercolor and
gouache on illustration board.
The display type was set in ITC Barcelona Medium.
The text type was set in Korinna.
Composition by Thompson Type, San Diego, California
Printed and bound by Tien Wah Press, Singapore
This book was printed on Leykam recycled paper, which
contains more than 20 percent postconsumer waste and has
a total recycled content of at least 50 percent.
Production supervision by Warren Wallerstein and Ginger Boyer
Designed by Joy Chu*

On the top of the Crumpetty Tree
The Quangle Wangle sat,
But his face you could not see,
On account of his Beaver Hat.

For his Hat was a hundred and two feet wide,

With ribbons and bibbons on every side

And bells, and buttons, and loops, and lace,

So that nobody ever could see the face

Of the Quangle Wangle Quee.

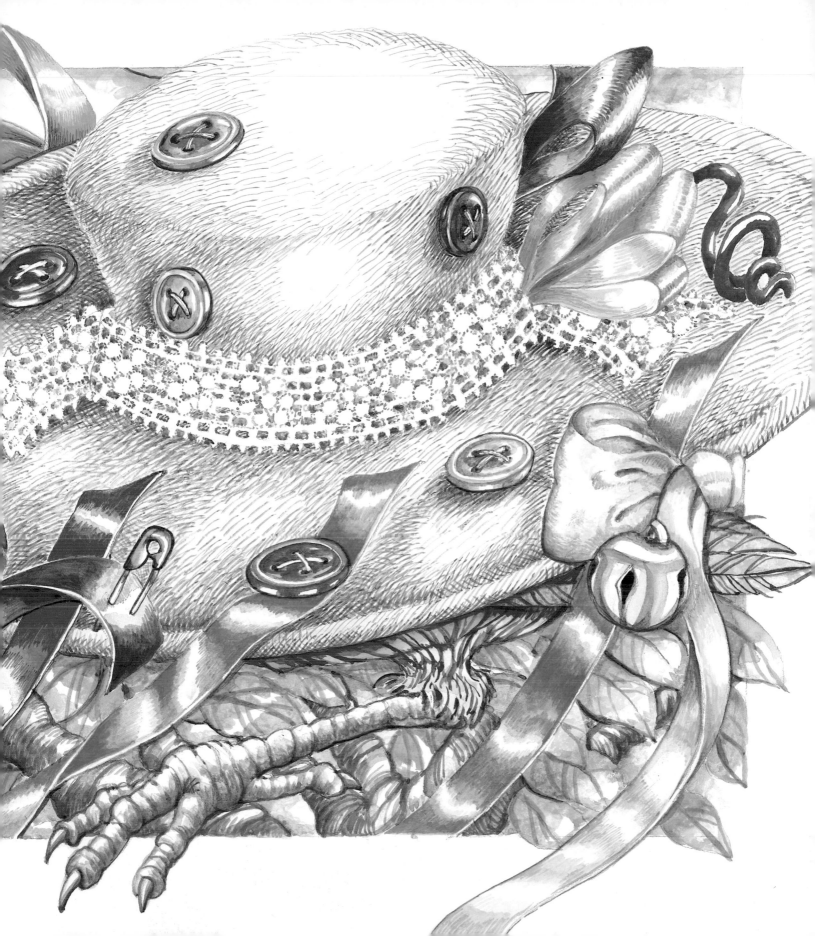

The Quangle Wangle said
    To himself on the Crumpetty Tree,—
"Jam; and jelly; and bread;
    Are the best of food for me!

"But the longer I live on this Crumpetty Tree
The plainer than ever it seems to me
That very few people come this way
And that life on the whole is far from gay!"
Said the Quangle Wangle Quee.

But there came to the Crumpetty Tree,
    Mr. and Mrs. Canary;
And they said,—"Did ever you see
    Any spot so charmingly airy?

"May we build a nest on your lovely Hat?
Mr. Quangle Wangle, grant us that!
O please let us come and build a nest
Of whatever material suits you best,
      Mr. Quangle Wangle Quee!"

And besides, to the Crumpetty Tree

Came the Stork, the Duck, and the Owl;

The Snail, and the Bumble-Bee,

The Frog, and the Fimble Fowl;

(The Fimble Fowl, with a Corkscrew leg;)

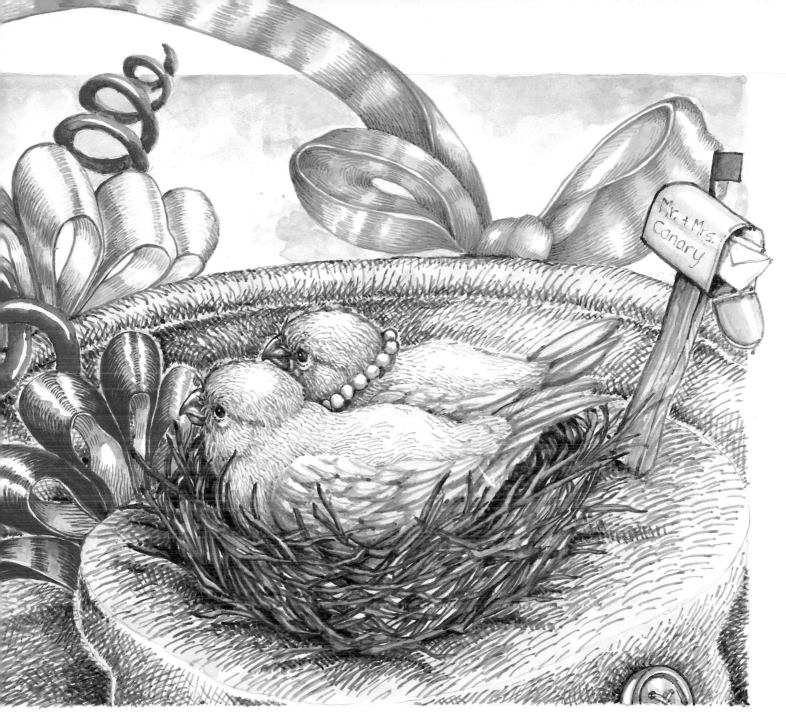

And all of them said,—"We humbly beg,

We may build our homes on your lovely Hat,—

Mr. Quangle Wangle, grant us that!

Mr. Quangle Wangle Quee!"

And the Golden Grouse came there,

And the Pobble who has no toes,—

And the small Olympian bear,—

And the Dong with a luminous nose.

And the Blue Baboon, who played the flute,—

And the Orient Calf from the Land of Tute,—

And the Attery Squash, and the Bisky Bat,—

All came and built on the lovely Hat
Of the Quangle Wangle Quee.

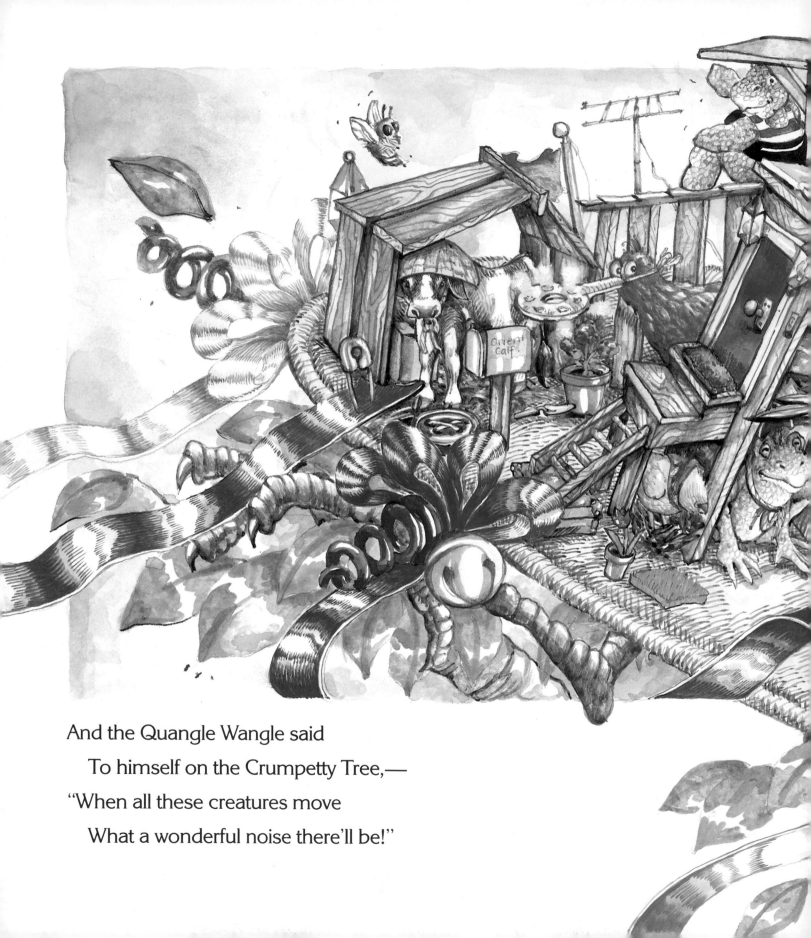

And the Quangle Wangle said
    To himself on the Crumpetty Tree,—
"When all these creatures move
    What a wonderful noise there'll be!"

And at night by the light of the Mulberry moon
They danced to the Flute of the Blue Baboon,
On the broad green leaves of the Crumpetty Tree,

And all were as happy as happy could be,

With the Quangle Wangle Quee.